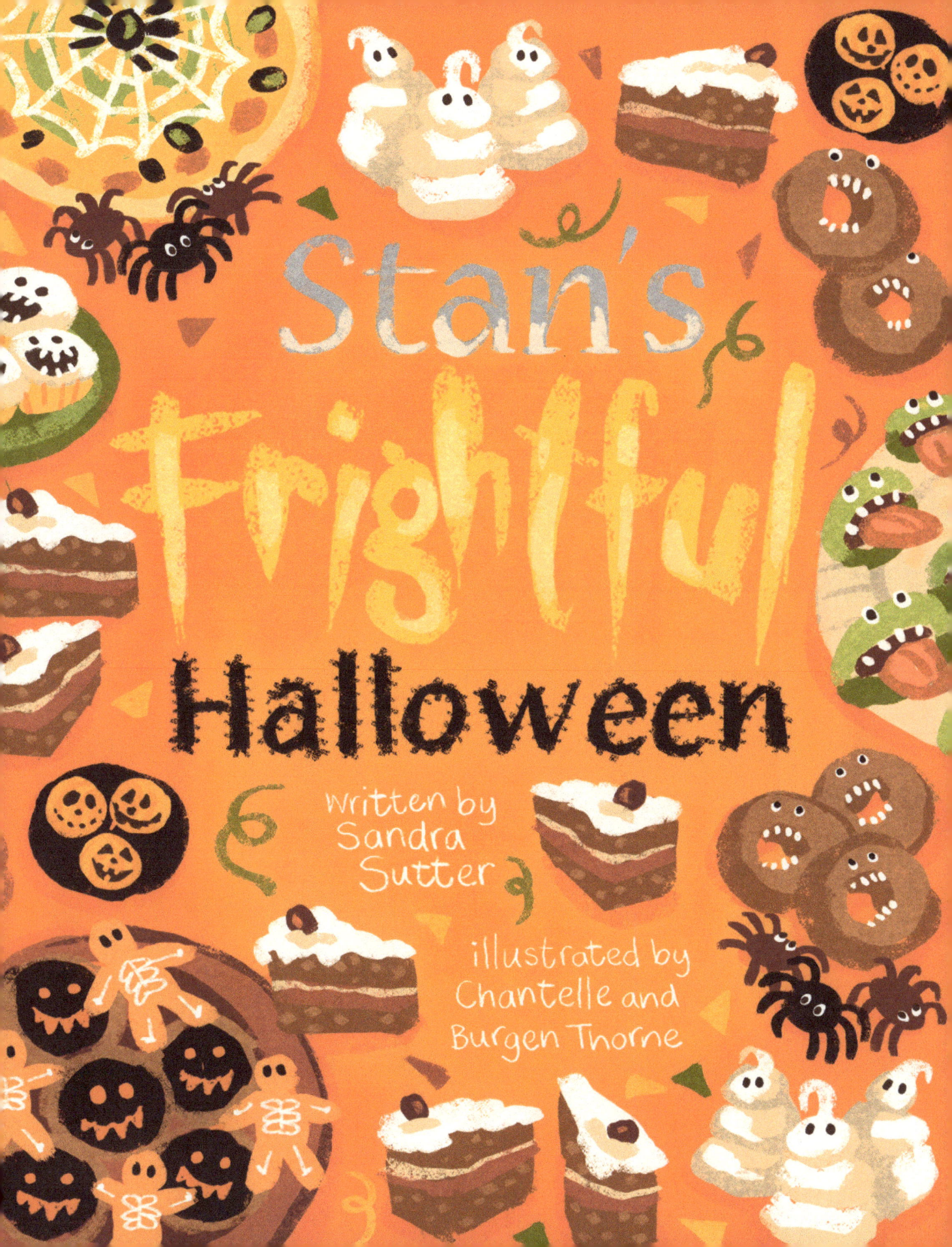

Please park all brooms at the door!

Stan's Frightful Halloween

written by Sandra Sutter
illustrated by Chantelle and Burgen Thorne

Stan always looked forward to Halloween. Being a werewolf, it was the one day each year he had permission to be as SCARY as he wanted.

Except...

Stan was also **clumsy**.

On the night before Halloween, he **fell** in the most awkward way.

Ouch!

"I broke my foot!" he wailed. "I can't keep up with the pack now."

So his friends went off **without** him.

Stan couldn't sit hopelessly at home alone.
He decided to try something new.

First, he went ghosting.
"How difficult can that be?"
Stan thought.

He wrapped himself
in rolls of **toilet paper**
and headed downtown.

Stan was a frightful sight. "Things can't go wrong this time," he thought.

That is, until …

SMACK!

He fell face first in the street.

Stan sighed.

Halloween was almost over and he hadn't scared anyone.

"I give up!" he declared and headed home.

Stan fell backwards into the door.

"AAAAACCCCKKK!" he howled.

Stan
stood up.

He saw his reflection in the mirror.

He looked

Frightful
Hideous
horrible

Within seconds, the entire room was filled with **monstrous laughter.** Stan joined his pack of friends as they gobbled up cake and candy.

It was a howling good time and the
best Halloween party ever!

Spider pizza

Use a frozen pizza base
Spread on tomato paste and add grated cheese
Make a spider web with cooked spagetti noodles
Create a spider in the middle using black olives. Use thin long slices for the legs
Sprinkle with your favorite toppings - pepperoni, mushrooms, green pepper - and bake. Easy peasy!!

Screaming donuts

Use your favorite donuts
Make teeth with ready rolled icing or white candy
Create eyes with circles of ready rolled icing and chocolate chips or use candy eyeballs
Add strawberry jam for details

Crazy cupcakes

Use plain cupcakes from your favorite bakery
Spread the top with strawberrry jam or dark chocolate spread
Cut rounds of ready rolled icing and cut out scary eyes and mouth, place on top so that the jam or chocolate spread shows through

Scary soda

Pour a glass of fizzy raspberrry soda
Use a toothpick or cocktail skewer to make an eyeball by putting together a raisin, a cocktail cherry and a litchi
Drop it into the soda and add ice

Stan's Frightful Halloween
Text Copyright © 2020 by Sandra Sutter
Art & design Copyright © 2020 by Chantelle & Burgen Thorne
Edited & Art Directed by Dr. Mira Reisberg
www.childrensbookacademy.com

All rights reserved. No part of this book may be reproduced in any form or by any electronic or mechanical means including information storage and retrieval systems - except in the case of brief quotations embodied in critical articles or reviews - without permission in writing from its publisher, Clear Fork Publishing.

Clear Fork Publishing www.clearforkpublishing.com
P.O. Box 870 102 S. Swenson Stamford, Texas 79553 (325)773-5550

Printed and Bound in the United States of America.
ISBN - 978-1-950169-38-2

When clumsy werewolf Stan breaks his leg on the eve of Halloween, he is heartbroken when his friends leave without him for what's sure to be a scary good time. But Stan isn't one to stay at home. Perhaps he can try ghosting? Or ride with the witches? After all, it can't be THAT hard.

Join Stan with his heart full of determination on this frightful Halloween adventure to see if his clumsy mishaps might lead to a surprisingly scary and satisfying end.

Visit www.sporkbooks.com to see more great kids' books.

To everyone with a little Stan in them.
And to the Dream Team for making
this another perfect pairing.

Sandra Sutter

Sandra Sutter has been waiting to share this frightfully fun story with the world since Stan stumbled into her imagination and took space in her heart. As a children's book author, she loves creating characters that all kids can relate to and root for. Sandra lives in the heart of Kentucky's Bluegrass region with her husband, two kids, two dogs with less charm than Stan, and an extraordinary cat that does ordinary things. Find out more about her at www.sdsutter.com.

With so much gratitude to all our friends and family for always being there for us - we love you guys!

Chantelle and Burgen Thorne

Illustrating as a duo is double the fun and the end result is always twice as satisfying. We love creating art together! The magic of children's books lies in the pairing of pictures and story, every word and every image is important. Ultimately, the book itself is also a shared experience between parent and child. It is our privilege and joy to create the illustrations for books like Stan - enjoy!
www.chantelleandburgen.com

Lightning Source UK Ltd.
Milton Keynes UK
UKHW020346260322
400619UK00002BA/109